Lucid America

By Aaron Paul Schaut

A Blue Max Publication

301 Alton Ave NE. Grand Rapids, MI 49503

Print ISBN: **979-8-218-33251-8**

For the victims.

Author Note

Lucid America is broken up into 3 Parts. The first and third parts are written from the point of view of Robert, while part two is written from the point of view of Crystal. I feel it's important to note this going in so that you don't waste any time being confused over the abrupt change in first-person characters.

Part 1

Robert, Not Bob

The Shingles

I stood there, staring up at a wall that divides the United States from Mexico. I stood there forever on a mountain, separating the United States from Canada. Alone in both locations and both require a long distance to return to people. The trips there are exciting and the trips back are boring.

Between the two points is a town called Columbus. Columbus is where I'm from. Columbus is the center of everything and the center of nothing. It was in Columbus that I bagged groceries, bussed tables, spread the shingles across the roofs—the American dream, shingles.

Now, I float around. I don't want to float around though. I want to be things that would be important to people important to me. With so many options, it's really hard to pick one thing. The mountain or the plain? The north has cold, the south has hot. So many options. They all have the same politics and so few options.

Columbus is where European people came to start a new life. Columbus is where slaves stopped while escaping the South. Columbus is where large government contracts took place. Now, it has a Starbucks and a Family Dollar and all the things required for an American to succeed. I walked away from

Columbus and all of its options. Too many options, even with the mall closing its doors. I walked all the way to the mountain and all the way to the desert. People didn't walk anymore, save for tracking steps on their watches.

Today, I'm standing on a corner in Winslow, Arizona. I know this because the mural on the wall tells me that this is where I am. It wasn't easy to get here. Along the way, I encountered frost, a friend, an enemy, and a bunch of in-betweens. It's the in-betweens that cause all the trouble. It's easy to see your friend, your enemy. The in-betweens have all the bad juju around them.

The Leaving

When I first left Columbus, I set up camp in Ashton. I had a desk surrounded by a padded wall with little windows on each side. I had post-it notes, pens, and a laptop computer with an extra monitor. Sometimes, at camp, there were snacks in a little kitchen, and coffee, and we had to fill out a form if we needed additional paperclips. There was a magnet with the name Robert Stonebrook printed on it, stuck to the side of my desk. This is my name. Still, a lot of people call me Bob. One guy calls me Bobby, but I've always preferred Robert.

Everyone was there every day at Camp Ashton, regardless of disaster or dreams. We can talk about Dennis Trombley, who was there every day, albeit more automated than during prior days. Word around the coffee maker said that his daughter had cancer. Every day he was at the camp, probably thinking about his daughter whose name was Emily. Trombley would say things about camp like, "It helps keep my mind off things," or, "You all keep me strong." We knew that on the inside he was dying. I figure that every second of every day at his desk was a lifetime or more of dying. Money, insurance. Steady, man. These are the options. Or, maybe these are the only options for Trombley. He looked tired, and his hair lost its color. These changes took place during all this time at the office, at camp.

Les Peterson, or maybe his name was Len, was getting a divorce. Maybe it was because his husband felt abandoned. Maybe he felt abandoned. Both of them spent all their time at an office. I don't remember Les, or Len, ever getting a big bonus or a raise; he worked very hard at the office, apparently, worked hard for a divorce, worked hard for loneliness, and worked hard to drive a decent car to and from his losses.

There was a woman named Pam. She was always there. She wore smart outfits although only in earth tones. She had those chains that ran from her glasses around her neck. She was also usually wearing a brooch of some kind. She probably wasn't super old, but man, she felt old. She clocked in before everyone and left after everyone else. She probably made the least money. She seemed like she was proud of everything she brought to the camp. Without the camp, I'm not sure she had a reason. Maybe she did. I never asked.

At Ashton, I survived off of a reward system. For every small and unsatisfying task, a cigarette or a cup of coffee or a snack from the snack box. Usually, all three. Sometimes, it was just a smoke. The term "reward" was a loose way of saying I was fucking dying along with everyone else, maybe more so. My eyes and my brain would fight the mundaneness and fucking pointlessness of all of it. Prison would at least allow my mind to run free, I think anyway. This was no prison; this was something else. Each click-clack of the keyboard, one of those beige, prison-colored keyboards, the keys a little dirty near their bottoms, was either unnoticeable or ear-piercing. The gray, Munsell gray bullshit everywhere blended with the dullness of it all.

Me, a company man? Maybe. It depends on how you look at it. I wasn't driven by success; rather, driven by fear. Each and every counterpart had a different sort of drive. For some, it was success. For others, it was fear. For most, it was just a job. For the 'just-a-job fellas,' it was the Bruce Springsteen, *Glory Days*, bullshit. They reeked of their glory days. Maybe I did too, but I don't remember having any glory days.

A December

December. I remember because they had decorations up—little bits of plastic garland and dull lights. Everyone had an anxious aura at the time. I felt a little closer to them, or they felt a little more like me, however you want to call it. A lot of the guys smelled like cologne mixed with a hint of brandy or whiskey. This was usually accompanied by glossy eyes and a bit of saliva on the strangely kept but also unkempt beard.

So, it was December. I didn't quit, and I wasn't fired. I was just gone. Middle of the day, I didn't bother with my things, just gone. I remember exiting the windowless lobby, through the metal door. The other side of the door was bright and blue and I felt like I just stripped down naked and let my skin feel the air. If I had a girl at the time, she wouldn't care, or I wouldn't care if she cared. Should I? Chances are she was either too put together or far, far from put together. I should say that the use of 'put together' isn't meant to be negative or insulting, just how they might appear to me, to be around me. My incapability to stand still probably had no match. I'd try, regardless, as a romantic.

The air touches my naked skin. It only took about a day to pack up and leave. Ashton wasn't my place, so, it had no claws.

I had no roots there. I could be anywhere in the world, and it would mean the same to me. As I drive away from Ashton, starting to feel remorse, I notice the small spiderwebbed chip in my windshield. I can't *not* focus on it and can also only focus on the seemingly muted *Heartbreaker* playing on the radio.

Heartbreaker. I can't remember the last time my heart was broken. What a dumb thing to say. Of course, I can remember the last time my heart was broken. It was only a couple of years ago and her name was Missa. At the time, I would have said she was the most beautiful girl in the world. Missa and I dated for a long time and she was just unbalanced enough to keep me on my toes. If I were to be honest, Missa really taught me how to fuck. I mean, you have sex, you make love, etc. Then, there is the world of fucking. This is brutal, no-holds-barred, talk-about-it-while-you-do-it, fucking. I really didn't like that part of her. It made me extremely nervous that anyone should be so bluntly into fucking. It didn't matter though. Every time she got undressed I'd lose complete control. Even after she put the noose around my neck and hung me out to dry, if she were here, right now in front of me, I'd have no control. In fact, we did a lot of fucking around right here in this van. I'm not sure what happened to Missa or where she is now. Considering how well things turn out for the bold ones, she's probably successful, married, kids. She probably beats the shit out of the lucky husband.

Speaking of the van, it's a conversion van from the 80s. It has these cool decals that run down the side—some graphic hangover from the 70s. It has captain's chairs and a bench seat that converts into a bed. It has fucking curtains. The point is, it has room for all my stuff that is loaded up and heading west. It's what you do, it's what comes naturally, you head west. I am heading toward the southwest.

The Bosses

The bosses are always here. The beatings I take from remorse or regret. I stop at a rest area outside Sedona, Twin Arrows to be exact. I set up camp here for a couple of days, waiting for an invitation. Laying down in the back of the van, in a parking lot, naked, is immensely erotic. You are in private and you are in public. The remorse and excitement and freedom combined with the cool sheets of the conversion bed leave me no choice but to feel it through. I come with hesitation but the passion is strong enough. The desert is foreign, and man, the stars flood the sky, the rocks a silhouette against the Milky Way light.

After washing up, I stare up into this orgy of cosmos and smoke a cigarette. I am wearing nothing but a pair of jeans. The running semi-trucks, lit up like boats, must think me a drifter. I am far from it. I am simply moving toward the next camp. I only have a little money and I would need to make decisions soon. At least a destination would afford me a starting point, a place to look for a job. I'd have to reach out to Ashton and convince them that I had to split. Some 'family emergency' should suffice. You wouldn't get far without a reference, but you know that. We all know that.

This is when it happened. I'm standing there in my jeans, taking a drag off my smoke, when the back of my head feels sharp and cold. Seconds pass, or maybe hours, and I open my eyes while my skin buzzes. I can hear the buzzing in my ears and feel it in my fingers. I get into the van and shut the door. The driver's side window is splattered with blood. I put my hand to the back of my head, and it is numb and stingy and cold. My hand is full of blood. I open the door and jump out in a panic. There is nobody around but the same stars, in a new position, and the humming tractor-trailers. Still reeling, I light a smoke, cough a little, and look around some more.

After I finish my cigarette, I head into the bathroom and the light, to assess the damage and clean up the blood. There is a ton of blood, typical of a head wound, or so I'd been told. I clean up the best I can and pick up my keys from the edge of the sink. I don't recognize the keychain. I do, however, recognize myself in the mirror. I have no real response to the unfamiliarity of the keys as I put them in my pocket and head back to the van. The keys did let me into the van so I guess they are mine. Hunching over and off-balance, I change into fresh clothes and put myself in the driver's seat. I can see that dawn is making an appearance in the rearview mirror. I am only about an hour from Sedona. I have the window down and am feeling a little faint. A single arrow, once a pair, stands tall as a reminder that the glory days of Route 66 were fading. The trading posts, filled with kachina dolls and beads and dream catchers, are still apparently strong. "Thai 66," one sign read.

The Wild West

Heading through a town called Kingman, I catch a glimpse of the Starbucks logo. I pull off of I-40 and into the drive-through, place my order, and slide up to the window. The barista hands me my drink and tells me my total. I go for my wallet. The wallet is gone. My heart sinks a little.

"I'm so sorry, my wallet is missing. I don't know what's going on. I think I was mugged at the rest stop."

"Oh no, I'm so sorry. Go ahead and take the coffee."

"If you don't mind, I'll stop inside and make some calls."

"No problem, see you inside."

I drive around and park. I notice the landscape of desert hills popping out above all of the retail signage. I dig into a small cubby in the back of the van and pull out my laptop. I set myself up at one of the tables in the Starbucks outdoor space and plug in. There is nobody here, so I light a cigarette. I call the banks and the credit card people and cancel all the things. I inquire about money with my bank. There is a branch about a mile from me, and they can help. I need a rest. I need to see a doctor. I need to call the police. Running on automatic, I do all of these things.

I check into a budget motel called Hilltop. A shower and a rest would feel luxurious right now. I set my duffle on my bed and step outside for a smoke. There is a couple speaking German a couple of rooms down. The man keeps glancing at me as they argue. I'm not sure why.

Unable to relax, I light another smoke. A rather robust woman approaches me from the left. I turn away, hoping not to engage in conversation. Unfortunately, no dice.

"Name's Pat. This is my place. You look a little rough for ware, pal. What's brought you to Kingman?"

"Hey Pat, name's Robert, I'm heading out west and ended up taking a pit stop here. Good to meet you."

"Good to meet you, Bob. What the hell happened to your head?"

"Robert. I was mugged at the rest stop up at Twin Arrows. The guy got me from behind. Took my wallet."

"Bob, I can't tell you how many times a guy got me from behind and took me for what I'm worth. Too many times to count. Oh well, keep the room clean, Bob. Goodnight."

"Goodnight, Pat."

She wandered back toward the motel office. I finish my smoke and head into my room. I remove my clothes and set them on the bed. I notice that the pendant, a pendant that was given to me by my mother, is gone. In the bathroom mirror, I look especially naked without it. I step into the shower and the water runs over my butterfly stitches. I let the remaining blood run down my body and into the drain. I spend about forty-five minutes just letting the warm water cover me. I should have never left. I should have stayed in my place, safe and secure. I should have just left well enough alone. I should have just kept fucking Missa and eating tacos and going to shows and doing the same old shit. Would I be better off? Maybe. I think about the drive to and from work. I think about how it seemed like one day bled into the next. In a way, I traded blood for blood. I laugh out loud at this thought. At the end of the day, it's neither here nor there. I'm here, that's there.

Exhausted, I turn on the television and fall asleep.

The Ache

The next morning, this morning, I wake up aching. I quickly get dressed, check my stitches in the mirror, and head outside for a smoke and to find a cup of coffee. The desert air feels right, though a little chilly. I have already decided to spend another night here as I think my body requires it. I decide that I'll head into town today. I'm here and it seems like it might be neat to check this little place out. I run back into the room to grab a couple of things and head back out to the van. I open up the side doors and drop my bag on the floor.

"Hey, cool ride." A voice came out of nowhere. Then, a figure appeared from around the van's side.

"Thanks," I respond while trying not to look startled. She looks to be about my age. Blonde hair, shoulder length with bangs. She is wearing a pair of dusty jeans and what looks like a vintage shirt with short sleeves and buttons and a tank top underneath. She wears a green pair of Chuck Taylors that look like they've survived a century.

"So, what's your deal?" She asks.

I shut the side door of the van. "Me? I'm heading west from Ashton. No deal, really."

"I'm heading west too! California! My car broke down on the highway and I'm just trying to figure it out. You're pretty cute, you want to have breakfast?

What? This sort of thing doesn't happen. I'm pretty cute? What the fuck is wrong with this girl? Clearly, this is a setup. Maybe that Pat woman set it up. She seems like the kind of woman who never minds her own business. Either way, I become a little high from the compliment and am already on this girl's string. It's a lucid high but a high nonetheless.

With only minor control, the words, "hop in," come out of me. I head around the passenger side and unlock the door. She jumps up into the passenger seat, bounces around a bit, and says, "Cool." I shut her door and she immediately rolls down the window. In this case, roll down is quite literal. I walk around to the driver's side and jump in. I also roll down my window and immediately go for a smoke.

"Do you know a place to eat?" I ask the girl.

"I've been here as long as you."

"Ah. Okay, we'll just look for something."

"You going to ask me my name?"

"I'm sorry," I reply, "I'm in a weird headspace today. What's your name?

"I'm Crystal, what's yours?"

"Robert. I don't go by Bob."

"Roger that, Bob." She's smirking. We pull out and scan for a breakfast dive. *Policy of Truth* is playing on the radio.

"So, Bob, why California? What's California got to offer you?"

"I don't know. Probably because it's where you go when you wanna go somewhere else. I mean, why not? I need to get out of middle American towns. What about you? What's California got to offer you?"

"Me, Bob?"

"Robert."

"I'm a loose cannon, Bob, that's what they tell me. I mean, I've had all the drugs; all the hyperactive drugs, all the antidepressants, all the bi-polar, tri-polar, polar-opposite, schizoid drugs. Like I said, I'm a loose cannon, Bob. That's what they say."

"Crystal, how about Mr. D'z?" I point at the diner to our right."

"Cool, man."

I pull into the parking lot and find us a spot. I step out and stand between a loose cannon and a dive breakfast.

The Used to Be

"I used to be a vegetarian, Bob."

"I see."

I can see she is attractive. I mean, I am attracted to her. I keep my responses to her energy to a minimum, but her energy is also attractive and also makes me high. It's a lucid high. I mean, I fucking wanted her the minute she floated out from around the van. I imagine her mouth pressed against mine. I imagine her little hand on my neck and running down my chest. I imagine all of the things that cause war and shotgun weddings. So, I keep my responses minimal. This is not to soften a disappointing blow. No... I am beyond that kind of thinking. It's simply because I don't really care. My neurons are firing, and my endorphins are surging, but this is just what happens when you're hit. Fucking cupid pulls out a bow and an arrow, and point blank puts a hole in you. She called me cute for Christ's sake.

"So you aren't a vegetarian, Crystal?"

"Not anymore."

"What are you calling yourself now?" Yes, I am also kind of an asshole.

"Fuck off, Bob. I started eating meat again because my fucking hair was falling out. I don't know why. It's just what fucking happened, Bob."

This is where I set myself up for love, see? By insulting her, now I feel bad about it. Now I'm going to put in the work to repair what I just did. Jesus.

"Bob, did you know that Twin Arrows used to be a part of Mexico? It was settled by Spaniards, Bob. You look like a Spaniard, Bob. Maybe I'll call you Roberto."

"I am not responsible for Twin Arrows, Crystal."

This whole conversation is taking place while we eat. I used to like eating and used to eat a lot. I don't care as much anymore. The consequences outweigh the gluttony. Crystal is eating a waffle with fruit and whipped creme on it. I also find this fucking attractive. She has a ring on every finger and her nails are cherry red.

"I wasn't implying you were. Just saying, you look kind of Spanish. You kind of remind me of that actor, Javier, from No Country for Old Men. That guy. You kind of look like that guy."

Slick as fuck, I pull a quarter out of my pocket and flip it onto the table, covering it with my other hand as it lands. "Heads or tails?" I ask with a smirk. She smiles a pretty big smile and squirms into a flirtatious pose. With this act, I salvage myself from my prior insult.

"Roberto, will you take me to California with you?"

What the fuck? What do I do with that? "What about your car?" is all that came out of my knucklehead mouth.

"I don't care about that car. It's a piece of shit. Let's go to California together, Bob. It'll be fun!"

I don't want to put logic to this. I could have said, "I don't even know you," or, "What if I'm a serial killer," but I didn't. Truth is, I immediately want it. If I sway her otherwise, I will regret it forever. She'll be another "one that got away."

"Probably, yeah," was all I had to say.

"Cool! Javier let's leave today. We can leave today, and we can make a road trip of it. What happened to your head, anyway?"

"Oh, yeah. Somebody mugged me at a rest area. Knocked me out and took some of my things. Put a little damper on my plans. I don't really remember. I was having a smoke and woke up with a bloody noggin and no wallet. It's mostly okay now."

"Fuck, man. That's crazy! That's the whole reason I always stay in those shitty motels. You hear about that happening. Fuck that guy. Should we find him and kill him?"

"We can make it a part of our plan. But, when we find him, I want to flip the coin."

We both laugh at this. We are synced.

The Radio

Crystal decides to take control of my radio on the way back to the motel. I can see that this is how this was going to play out. She digs up some pop station and sings along and dances in her seat. I watch her body move to the music out of my peripherals. This is nature. Halfway through the song, she turns the dial to a station playing mariachi. She checks herself in the side mirror. When she does this, I can sense something in her, like a thought landing on her nose that she notices, briefly reflects on, and swats away. Obviously, she is here for a reason, maybe several reasons. I am also here for a reason, maybe several reasons. I know that these places are what she's trying to avoid. So, I keep this intimacy to myself. She turns toward me and throws her feet onto my lap. I feel myself moving. She feels it too.

There is a piece of road between Mr. B'z and the motel that is desert-empty. Rocky behemoths jut out from the yellow and brown landscape. After feeling me move, she asks if we can stop. So, I pull the van off the side of the road. "Common," she says while opening the door.

I get out of the van and meet her at the edge of the landscape. She takes my hand and leads me up the dry and rocky hill. She leads me around large rocks and up the side of a small cliff. She holds my hand and points to the horizon. The sky transitions from a deep blue to a very light blue, not unlike her eyes. The cliffs and peaks jut into the sky while a slight breeze brushes our skin. She turns me, grabs the back of my head, and presses her lips into mine. She kisses me with the kind of passion you see in a movie. I put my arms around her and pull her in tight. Cars honk their horns, but for me, the sound is far away and has no effect on the scene. Maybe it does. If it were a movie, it would have added to the ambiance of the moment regardless.

Continuing to hold my hand, she leads me down the backside of the cliff. Behind the outcropping, she kisses me again. This time, her hand unbuttons my shirt. She pulls back and removes hers. She presses her breasts against my chest and kisses me slowly. She slides her hand into my pants and holds me, moving her hands softly, gently. She removes her hand and then removes her jeans. She pulls my jeans off and caresses my hip. Our naked skin is hot while pressed together. The breeze kisses us as it slides around any exposed surface. She puts her hands on my shoulders and pushes me down onto my jeans. She slowly sits on me, around me. I look at her flushed face and into her eyes. I last about a minute, maybe two minutes. She gets there too; I think anyway. I became buzzed up. I am floating. The whole fucking mountain is mine, is ours.

She hugs me tight and kisses me again after sliding her fingers through my hair. The scene repeated itself. Fucking twice.

The Hilltop

We pull into Hilltop. She kisses me and runs to her room for her things. I light a smoke and take a second to think. I didn't have long to think. She was back at the van in half a cigarette's time. I find myself excited and more-so anxious. I place my half-smoked cigarette in the small span between the hood and the fender. I tell Crystal that I'll be right back and run into my room to get my things. I hadn't really unpacked my bag, so it only took a few minutes. I run back out and into the parking lot. She isn't there. I call out for her, but she doesn't answer. I pull my almost-gone smoke out of its makeshift holder and take a final drag. I should have known she'd split. When two souls combine at such a massive rate, they are sure to supernova. Perhaps this result is more a fear of a supernova. Either way, I had a feeling it was too good. I stare toward her room. I hear my new name. "Javier, I grabbed some sodas and chips from the office." Okay. Supernova resume.

We jump in the van.

Passing the 'love cliff' turns me on. I want to stop and do it all over again. I think she could feel me reeling as she digs her nails into my thigh. She is staring at me. I look at her and give her a wink.

"Where we headed now?" she asks.

"Barstow."

"How long? Are we there yet?"

"A few hours."

There are only telephone poles and desert bushes and faded hills. Crystal's feet are up on the dash and she's focusing through the horizon. A Santa Fe train is running alongside the van. We cross the state line and the Colorado River. We are in California. I feel it, she feels it. This is one step closer to a destination that we apparently share.

R.E.M.'s *End of the World* comes on the radio for some reason. This puts a surge through my companion's nervous system. She cranks the volume knob up, dances in her seat, and rattles off every single word. I've never known a single person to sing every single word of that song. She even turns on the CB radio and sings into the microphone. I'm not sure anyone can hear her, but if they can, they might be pushing down a little harder on the gas pedal. The whole thing is pushing me to push down on the gas pedal. I even sing the chorus with her. She seems inebriated by the whole Stipe-driven van party. I feel mostly separated from it.

The song closes out which leaves us both in an awkward state of "what next." The "what next" is quickly broken by

Crystal.

"Let's get something to eat!" she says as we come upon the town of Needles.

"Yeah? Are you hungry? Let's see what they have here."

We exit 40, and I navigate the van toward The Mother Road. There are crudely painted murals of the 66 signs everywhere. Crystal spots some eye candy in the form of a building, fully muralized in airbrush, that serves pizza. She points and hops around in her seat, so I pull the van into a parking space. We seat ourselves underneath a mural of a '57 Chevy that reads "America's Love Affair." We both sit next to each other. I wanted her again.

We order our pizza and some Cokes and start what seems like a very natural conversation. It starts with Crystal asking me where I am from.

"Where am I from? I don't really remember. I mean, I guess I do. I was born in Ohio, near Columbus. My family traveled, moved around a lot, mostly in the Midwest. What about you?"

"I'm from Wisconsin, grew up in Milwaukee."

We eat and talk about Milwaukee. She talks about the lake and the food and the people until we are done eating. We head up to pay the check. Crystal insists, and I insist. Through all of the insisting, Crystal's bag falls to the floor.

It's funny how the minute that things seem to become legitimately normal, a fucking meteor screams through the air and lands right in your fucking lap.

As I bend over to help her pick up her bag and her things, I spot on the floor my wallet and the pendant my mother had given me. She sees that I see. She knows that I know. I pick up the pendant and the wallet. She looks into my eyes; I look into hers, but only briefly. I stand up and walk outside and into the street. I walk through a parking lot and onto another street. I walk until there is a fence. I hop over the fence and cross the highway. I can sense Crystal following. I walk into the desert and over the top of a cement pad painted up with the Route 66 sign and a roadrunner. I walk over it, walk over an old chunk of road, and into more desert.

She is still following me. I walk around little subdivisions via the sand and just keep going until there are no more houses. I walk for about an hour until I reach a canyon. I stop walking and sit on a rock. I am only looking forward and don't look back, but I can feel her making her way toward me. I can feel she is still quite far behind. The landscape looks like something from *Gunsmoke*, or *Star Trek*, maybe from Mars. I can hear her approaching now. Because of this, I am not startled when I feel her hand on the back of my neck. The shivers that run down my spine are either caused by desire or by anger, which one, I am not really sure at this point. I feel her lips kiss the back of my neck. After this, her hand runs around my shoulder as her body follows. She stands over me, in front of me, looking down at me. I look up at her, but she is only a silhouette in the sun. She grabs my head and pushes my face into her stomach. I can smell her essence. "Do you hate me?" she asks. How fucking cliché. I don't even know how to respond. She crouches down and kisses me on my lips and on my face. I don't react but regardless, all my neurons are firing. I set my things down on the ground, and we fuck. The whole thing is intense. We stay there, lay there, for hours. I never say a fucking word.

The Clouds

My vision had been cloudy as far back as I can remember. Not my literal vision, but rather my ability to focus on things around me. I've never actually looked at things, people, tiles in the tub. I've always just felt like I was looking through everything, retaining almost nothing. Or, at least, retaining just enough information to remain in the present, scrape by, aware enough to go through the motions of working, eating, shopping, and getting coffee. Sometimes I'd tell myself to look at things. When I did this, my surroundings became unfamiliar or, maybe, familiar on a different plane of emotional bondage. It was like seeing something you might despise. Maybe, it is like seeing something for what it is but despising how you ended up there. My ability to predict, or care to predict outcomes, was fading. This made it harder to change course. Changing course was a way of always seeing everything new and unblemished by past transgressions or stupidity. Here I am, at this table, drinking coffee. None of this is real, all of it is real.

Crystal and I walk back through the desert to the van. Neither of us says a word. Maybe I've lost my hearing. She gets in, I get in. We drive toward Barstow, and I pull off at Barstow and into the parking lot of Motel 66. I remove my things from the van while Crystal stays in her seat. I get a room and enter the room and sit on the bed. Shortly after, Crystal enters the room. She puts her bag on the table and sits next to me.

Everything starts shaking. The bed, the walls. The coffee maker hops off the side of the table, the microwave hops off the mini-fridge. We are both looking into each other's eyes. Car alarms start firing off and you can hear sirens in the distance. The whole thing lasts about 30 seconds. I have never felt anything like it. Total loss of control. A claustrophobia of sorts consumes me. At the same time, it reminds me of the trains going by the house in Columbus. Crystal has tears in her eyes. I don't think it's the quake that is causing the tears. I don't know how to not care. I kiss her eye.

"Can we take your van into the desert?" Crystal asks.

"What do you mean?" I am hesitant to talk. My voice seizes up a little when I do.

"I want to spend some time in seclusion. I want to spend some time in seclusion with you."

"I don't know." I really don't know.

"Please think about it."

I stand up and slip outside for a cigarette. The day had become night. There are mild tremors every so often. I stare at the sky. Crystal peeks at me through the curtains. I head up to the window and yell that I'd go find us coffee. She nods through the pane. I know that she wonders if I'll come back. I also wonder if I'll come back. I know I will. It's my nature.

The Passion

My body is hurting from depression and from being overwhelmed with excitement. I can never tell if this is how I'm meant to be. When I don't feel these things, I crave them, find them, create them. Without them, I am dead. Maybe it has more to do with love than anxiety. Maybe it's a simple word like codependence. Maybe it's a simple word like bananas or psychotic or something-polar. Maybe it's passion. I've always preferred the word passion to any other word. For me, this is an undeniable truth. I exist; therefore, I must be passionate. If I stop feeling passion, then I stop living. This is probably where sex and love come into play, the purest and most organic and innate form of passion. Animal fucking passion.

Of course, we can take the van into the desert. Of course, I can't deny myself or resist the potential for this unknown passion. It'll probably hurt. This is where I am probably meant to be. So, fuck it! We'll take the van into the desert.

I walk back into the motel room. Crystal had fallen asleep while I was outside. She looks small, innocent. I lay down next to her and put my hand on her stomach. She presses her head in between my arm and my chest. It didn't take me long to join her in sleep.

The Painted Desert

I felt the light cross my eyelids. It didn't take long for ideas to wake me full up. I can hear Crystal in the shower. I imagine her body, water running down her skin. I get up and step out for coffee. I walk back into the room and find Crystal pulling her jeans up around her waist. "Thanks," she says as I hand her a coffee. I smile, but I'm not talking yet. I throw my things into my bag and step back outside and to the van. A few minutes pass and she joins me. I get up and into the driver's seat and she gets into the passenger seat. I start the van and we head out.

Up the road I stop for gas, smokes, and essentials. While pumping the gas, Crystal tells me she'll get the essentials. "Make sure you get a ton of water," I tell her. She nods on her way through the parking lot. I'm done pumping gas and notice her carrying all the things. I run over and grab the water. We pack everything into the van. She mentions that she forgot something and jets back into the store. About a minute later, she runs out, tells me to get in the van as she gets into the van. "Let's go man," she says. I feel her urgency and I know why.

I move the van quickly onto Main. We watch civilization disappear as we find ourselves on National Trails Highway. We come to a crossroads of sorts. "This is it," Crystal says. I turn off and we drive down a dirt path, into the guts of the Mojave.

"I love you," she says.

The foothills of the Sierra Nevada look like a scene from M*A*S*H. We park the van near the bottom of one of these small hills. "Let's go!" Crystal says. She grabs some bottles of water and her bag from the back of the van and starts walking up the hill. I grab a pack and follow.

We don't venture too far when she says, "right here." I go into my pack and pull out a sheet that I was using for the conversion bed. I spread it out in the sand. We both look for small bits of brush and wood to build a fire. There is the remnants of a building or shack near us, and I gather some old boards from its remains. I return to her, sitting on the sheet, starting the small fire. I place my wood on the ground and sit down next to her, lighting a cigarette. After several minutes of silence, she breaks it.

"I'm sorry."

"Me too. What the fuck did you hit me with?"

She reaches into her bag and pulls out a .38 revolver. "I hit you with this."

"You hit me with the butt of a gun? Are you fucking kidding me? Like something out of some cop movie?"

"Exactly like something out of a cop movie."

"Did you rob that gas station back there in Barstow?"

She pulls a handful of bills out of her bag and shows them to me. She places them into my hands. I can't tell if she's looking for approval or what. She then pulls a bottle of Tequila from her bag and opens it. She takes a drink and hands me the bottle. I take a drink. She quickly kisses me and pulls away; her stare remains. I grab her head and pull her in. We are still in the throes of a passion. We are turned on by each other, our transgressions, our fear, and our fire. The fire won't fade quickly, if at all. After releasing ourselves of several hours of silence and a building up of tension, we sat naked, save for a blanket, and sipped on the tequila while staring at the fire. The sky served as a perfect backdrop as the sun faded.

I crawl over and put some more of the old wood on the fire.

"Let's get drunk," she says. She takes a large swig from the bottle and hands it to me. I take a large swig.

"How'd you end up here?" I ask her.

"We drove?"

"We did. I mean, how the fuck did you end up becoming you, becoming this?" I handed her the bottle.

"That's a long fucking story." She took another swig and

handed the bottle back.

I took another drink and found myself spinning. I stood and looked down to find that Crystal had laid down on the blanket with her eyes shut. I took the bottle and walked a little way out into the hills. The Milky Way was so visible that I had no trouble finding my way. Unfortunately, looking up to the heavens left me bent over, purging myself of what felt like several liters of Tequila. I make my way back to our camp, drink some water, and lie down next to her.

The Mourning

I wake to a blistering sun. My body still wants to expel last night's daemons. I start to open my eyes, excited to see her face next to me. Instead, while barely conscious, I can make out some stitching and straps and what turns out to be my duffle bag. I become fully detoxed and reach over to pat down her side of the sheet. There is no body. I open my eyes to a squint, sit up, and look around. My heart sinks and my soul is crushed. There is no van, there is no Crystal.

Part 2

Crystal

The Leaving

I watched him stand there, staring up at a wall that divides the United States from Mexico. I watched him stand there, forever, on a mountain, separating the United States from Canada. Alone in both locations and both require a long distance to return to people. The trips are a lot of work for him. I can only see him from afar.

I sat on the chair watching Tommy playing video games. There was somebody at the other end of his headset, probably also using words like "dope" and "dawg" and shouting "Eat a dick" and "Fuck you." I had probably been here for a millennium, it felt like a million years, sitting here, watching Tommy trash-talk the people on the other side of the headset. When he saw me thinking, he'd say things like, "Yo, s'alright baby, we gots big things on the horizon." Of course, I didn't believe him, he's said this for a trillion years. It didn't matter though. I wasn't going to survive. I've also spent the last million years with doctors and shrinks and with pills and with other pills. All the doctors and shrinks were highly recommended and very good at their jobs. They'd just 'switch it up a little, make little adjustments.' Close monitoring would allow me to live a 'completely normal life.'

It was December. I remember it this way because the

restaurant was all dolled up with garland and glitter and the windows were covered in snow spray paint. We had a lot of regulars. Some were great, others were not, and some were in-between. The in-between customers are the worst. You might get treated okay, but the tips wouldn't suggest that you did a good job. They might treat you like garbage and leave a big tip while mentioning your poor services in an online review. At least you could recognize an asshole, or an honest to god nice person. Those two types allowed you to react naturally.

So, I'm sitting here watching Tommy play his fucking video games, promising big things. It becomes as though I am on autopilot, I go into our room and throw some of my things into a bag and I throw Tommy's gun into my bag. I open our window and slide through to the outside. I go to our shitty car and get in. I back out of the driveway before turning on the lights. I just leave.

I start out toward Chicago and think about the weather. The cold and wind easily push me into thinking bigger. I still move toward Chicago. Where do people go when they split? They go to California. Fuck yeah, California.

The Bosses

The bosses are always here. The years I spent taking orders. The tickets and the boyfriends and the customers and friends. The toll it all takes on my soul. I would have thought that after so many smiles, listening to so much ego, sucking so much dick, that I'd at least be in a place to give orders rather than take them. I shouldn't say that. What I mean is, I want to feel free. I want the freedom to think and feel and search for myself. It doesn't seem possible. I'm always so busy serving others that I can't breathe. It seems like the only time I'm able to be free is while I sleep. I dream myself away, somewhere else, somewhere where I'm recognized as more than just an ego microphone or fuck hole. If I had to have Tommy on top of me one more time, I'm not sure I'd make it through the night, or he wouldn't. So, I've made it to Twin Arrows where I stop at a rest stop to wash up and rest up, a little.

I managed to sleep a little before washing up in the restroom. I had little money and gave little thought to what that meant. I gave a lot of thought to what that meant when I got back to the car. Ready to leave, the car won't start. I turn the key several times. Sometimes, it almost sounds like it's going to start but never does. I get out of the car frustrated. I kick the door shut and quietly scream at it. I scan the parking lot. There is a man, a shirtless man, walking out of the restroom and heading toward their vehicle. Instinct kicks in. I reach into my bag and grab Tommy's gun. The man is standing outside his vehicle smoking a cigarette. I sneak around his vehicle and up behind him and hit him in the head with the butt of the gun, like they do in the movies. He drops to the ground. I didn't expect him to drop to the ground. I thought for sure that I would have little impact on him, and he'd beat the shit out of me. I can take a beating. In this case, I don't have to. I take his wallet; it has some solid bills in it. Around his neck and over his naked chest, he is wearing what looks like a silver pendant. It's full of turquoise and looks handmade. I slowly take it off of him. I head to the truckers, one who is leaving, and hitch a ride.

"Name's John, what's yours?" the trucker asked as I settled into his cab.

"Names Becky," I told him my name was Becky. It's a stupid fucking name but it would do fine for now.

"Becky, hey? I dated a Becky once. She preferred Rebecca but I called her Becky anyway. Didn't last long."

"Huh," was my only response.

"Where you headed, Becky?"

"A motel?"

"Tell you what, I'm heading to a motel I often stay at. It's just up a little way, place called Hilltop. Will that work for you?"

"Sounds good, John. I really appreciate the ride."

"No good deed."

No good deed was a good sign. It was a simple way of saying, 'I'm not going to rape you or expect you to fuck me.' This guy must be somebody's dad, in a good way.

"How come you're hitchin' a ride? Something happen back there at the rest area?"

"My car broke down. I'd rather just get somewhere and sleep. I'll deal with the car tomorrow."

"That's a good enough reason. Just glad it isn't some kind of thing, some kind of trouble. I been clean for about two years. I need to stay that way. Easiest way to do that is by steering clear of trouble, if you know what I mean."

"I do. I like you, John. Thanks for telling me that."

We pull off of the exit at Kingman and shortly after into the parking lot at Hilltop. The hotel has a cool old neon sign and looks quaint and quiet.

"This is perfect, John," I say as I open the door of his rig.

"Okay, Becky. My truck will be parked in front of my room. You need anything, just knock."

"Thank you," I say and hop down to the parking lot. I check

into a room and fall asleep while staring at the pendant I'd taken

from the guy at the rest stop. I feel somehow connected to it.

The Wild West

I didn't wake up to the thrill and excitement of a road trip. I was concerned about where I was, and how I'd get where I was going. I needed to figure out how to keep moving. I sit on the hotel bed thinking about the distance I put between myself and my life in Wisconsin. I count the money from last night. A few hundred bucks. I decide that I should get some breakfast and look at some options. If there was one thing I wasn't, it was in a hurry.

Leaving the room, I notice that John's truck is gone. He didn't try to rape me or take advantage of me. I half wished he was still here. He'd probably buy me breakfast if he was. He was a nice man.

I walk a few blocks and discover a small diner. The sign says to seat myself, so I seat myself. A nice woman takes my order and I order a coffee and an orange juice. I order a small breakfast. I look to my phone for advice. I take my pills with my orange juice. I really don't have much to go on. Tommy had called several times. To say several times would be putting it lightly. He called about a hundred times. There are thirty-two voicemails and about two-hundred text messages. The last message, the only one I look at, simply says, "I'll kill you, bitch."

This isn't hurtful or scary or anything. It doesn't mean anything to me.

I walk back to the hotel, lie on the bed, and watch TV. I need to rest my head for a while. I watch Die Hard and Die Hard 2. I step out of the hotel and get some sodas from the soda machine. I head back into my room and take a shower. The water feels good on my skin. I'm enjoying a Coke in the shower. It tastes extra fizzy and feels cool as I press the can to my chest and forehead. Wearing a towel, I lie back down on the bed and watch the Lethal Weapon movies until I fall asleep. This is all okay. I've been exhausted for twenty-some years.

The Ache

I woke up in the morning with an ache in my heart. For whatever reason, I feel remorse for leaving. I tell myself that I need to not feel remorse. I will need a distraction to keep myself from reeling. Not that there wasn't enough to be distracted about. I needed a vehicle. I needed to get my car or something. I need some coffee if I'm going to think. I head outside and am immediately thrown by the van parked nearly right in front of my room. I see him standing there. He's having a cigarette. His back is to me just like it was the other night. Remorse fills my heart again. I'm not exactly sane when it comes to matters like this.

"Cool ride," I say. What the fuck is wrong with me. "So, what's your deal?" He is cute. I would have never wondered how he was doing had he not shown up here. I ask him what his deal is. He tells me he's from Ashton and heading west. These are the magic words, heading west. I tell him about my car. I tell him I'm also heading west. "You're pretty cute," I tell him. "Let's get breakfast."

It was a strange feeling to be up in his van. I felt like a spy or some kind of intruder. I also felt a gush of excitement over all of it. He seems pretty nice and is definitely good-looking. I can feel him checking me out as we drive. I can feel his nervousness. What if this was some kind of fate? What if this was some kind of destiny? I wonder how long it will take for him to start telling me what I need to do. Maybe I should tell him what he needs to do.

"What's your name?" He asks me. I tell him my name is Crystal. He tells me his name is Robert, but he doesn't go by Bob. I immediately start calling him Bob. I guess I'm flirting. What the fuck?

I ask him why California. He tells me it's because it's where you go. I can agree with that.

"I'm a loose cannon, Bob. That's what they tell me. I mean, I've had all the drugs; all the hyperactive drugs, all the antidepressants, all the bi-polar, tri-polar, polar-opposite, schizoid drugs. Like I said, I'm a loose cannon, Bob. That's what they say."

"Crystal, how about Mr. Dz?" He points at the diner to our right."

"Cool, man." I'm easy like that.

He pulls into the parking lot. I feel my remorse turn its head a little bit. It'd be ironic if he bought me breakfast.

The Used to Be

"I used to be a vegetarian, Bob."

"I see," is all that he says. He must think he's a James Dean type. He messes with me a little about the vegetarian thing. He's being kind of a dick. It's not terrible. At least it lacks ego. It's more of a beat-down, semi-intelligent sort of a dick. He also kind of looks like Javier Bardem, which doesn't hurt.

We talk about where we are, this is where I'm at. It's small talk. I tell him about the Spaniards and Twin Arrows and tease him a little more about his name. I start calling him Roberto. He seems receptive to my humor. That doesn't happen often. I mean, I think I'm funny, fun. Tommy mostly wanted to talk about his thing.

The customers at the restaurant seem to like me sometimes. I know that I have a kind of odd sense of humor. Some people are offended by me. I'm not sure why.

During our breakfast, still talking about the Spaniards, I tell him that he looks like Javier Bardem. It's really fucking cute that he takes a quarter out of his pocket and asks me to call it. He doesn't know that 'No Country for Old Men' is one of my favorite movies. There is a certain warmth to that movie. I fucking love it.

Me being me, this fucking string of words comes out of my mouth, "Roberto, will you take me to California with you?" What the fuck am I thinking? I mean, is my desperation and the fact that I kind of like this guy going to put me right back into the control of another man? That is *not* how I want to go out. What the fuck is wrong with me?

Surprisingly, all he says is, "What about your car?" all I say is that it's a piece of shit and that I don't care about it. Clearly, I am not in control of myself here. I'm not sure who is. Maybe it's the Spaniard. They have a way about them.

Now I am determined. I've settled into the idea that Robert and I are going to California together. Good thing I didn't steal his van. I probably should have stolen his van. I need to get the robbery out on the table.

"What happened to your head?" I ask him.

"Somebody mugged me at the rest stop." Fuck, I thought for sure this might trigger some memory of me, of my face.

"Let's find the mother fucker and kill him," I say with my signature smirk.

He smiles a shy little smile.

I think this guy really likes me.

The Radio

I decide to take over his radio. Most guys hate this. I mean, I have never met a guy that didn't hate this. I put it on the pop station and sing and dance around. I can feel him digging me. I'm actually pretty flattered and a little turned on by it. This guy might actually like me for me, even this me, dancing to pop music. I turn the station to some Mexican Mariachi station. Again, with the remorse, maybe fear, I sink into myself in the side mirror. I let the air come in through the window and brush against my hair and face. I can feel that he can feel my depression. I don't want him to see this in me. I want him to like me for me, not because he feels pity for me. I'm never going to be anybody's sick puppy again.

I force myself out of the darkness and throw my feet onto his lap. I brush against his cock and feel him get semi-erect. I let the enthusiasm and anxious excitement control me and ask him to stop the van. He does. Both sides of the road are vacant desert. A small hill of rock and dirt.

"Common," I tell him. I take his hand and lead him up the hill. The sky might be the most beautiful sky I'd ever seen. I can feel us. Still, under the control of what the drugs fail to control, I grab his neck and kiss him. I can feel his kiss in my toes. The cars are honking at us. I fucking love it.

It's unusual for me to want to do this. I want to say that this is not only a very obvious attraction, paired with the fact that I recently messed this guy up, but an obvious fuck you to my life before now. The idea of it all has me wet.

I grab his hand and lead him to the backside of the hill. I'm going to fuck him. Not only did I mess him up, but he also messed me up, twice. He is passionate, gentle, and we make love.

The Hilltop

Back at the motel, I kiss Robert and head to my room to grab my things. I can't fucking believe this is happening. I'm still warm and flush from making love on the hill. I'm going to go with this guy to California. I have a partner. As long as I don't let him become anything but a partner. I don't need another leader. I need a friend. I'd love a friend. It's not like I've ever had any real friends. I'd either not been allowed, or they bored the fuck out of me. I mean, people are fucking assholes. Did I take my pills? Fuck, I can't remember. Fuck. I think I did. I bet he'd like it if I grabbed some snacks for the road.

I think I made him nervous. He seemed nervous when I got back to the van. We hit the road. As we pass our little mountain, I feel the heat coming off of him. I get a little turned on by it and dig my nails into his thigh. I'd probably do the whole thing again right now. He tells me we are heading to Barstow. I settle into the hypnotic views of the desert. I start thinking about what I did to this guy. Is this okay? How come I don't feel sad about it? Is it because it led us here? Is what I did a good thing? Is this just an excuse that my messed-up mind made up to push away any remorse? The other side of excitement is a sadness that my body tries very hard to bury. Look at this place. I'd never seen anything like it. Dirt and browns and oranges and little weird desert bushes. R.E.M. pulls me out of this funk. It's cute that Robert is trying to sing along. I know all of the words to this song. Good luck keeping up, Chuck. I'm having fun. I can't remember the last time I had fun. Just fun. After all of it, I'm hungry.

"Let's get something to eat!"

"Yeah? Are you hungry? Let's see what they have here."

We drive into this little town. We are back on Route 66. I'm a sucker for all of it. There is this pizza place all painted up like some kind of street graffiti.

"We gotta go there!" Robert pulls into the pizza place. It's fucking cool! We talk about where we are from. It feels so normal, so adult. When we are finished, he tries to pay. I insist on paying. The little 'couple's squabble' finds my bag on the floor, contents spilled out. His fucking wallet is right there, so is his necklace. Fuck me.

I look into his eyes. I can see he's completely and totally messed up. He stands up and walks outside. I gather up the things, toss the woman at the counter some money, and follow him out of the restaurant. I stop. Maybe he needs a little space. Maybe I need to let him go. Maybe I should fucking end myself right here and now. He's just walking away. I just follow him. My heart is aching, and I feel the tears start to run down my face.

I'm shaking and trying to keep up with him. I'm not sure how far we are walking. I don't care.

We are well away from everyone and everything.

He stops and sits down. I want to embrace him. I'm finally up on him and put my hand on his neck. I wasn't sure what he was going to do. He didn't really move so I kiss him on his neck and move around to face him. Shaking, tears in my eyes, tears in his, I press his face against my stomach.

"Do you hate me?" I didn't have any words. *Any words* would have been stupid. My voice is trembling. He doesn't respond. Knowing that any words are stupid, I kiss him on his lips and on his face. His lips send shivers through my soul. He strips off my clothes and I strip off his clothes. We never stopped kissing through all of it. As he enters me, I can feel him through my whole body. I shake and convulse while we kiss and come together. Afterward, we lay there. I still don't have any words. I don't think he does either.

The Clouds

When I don't take my medication, I can't always distinguish between good feelings and bad feelings. I'm not one hundred percent sure I believe this. I've been told this by several different people. I know that my reaction to the things around me can make total sense to me regardless of the good, or the bad. I become overwhelmed often. Overwhelmed with a strong desire to leave, overwhelmed with a strong desire to explode, overwhelmed with a strong desire to implode. When they play that noise in the movies, the high-pitched noise that a character hears after a bomb goes off, this is how it feels. Like my thoughts and my body and my life are muted by an almost deafening high-pitched ringing. You want it to go away, but it doesn't. You can feel it in your skin, under your skin. There is nothing you won't do to get away from everything so that you have some sense of control. Similarly, the sound of a tornado siren gives me total control. The exhilaration of it makes me feel like I'm invincible. Maybe this is what drives people to be test pilots or climb mountains. Maybe I like it. Maybe I like things messed up.

I walk back to the van with Robert. A long, silent walk through the desert. We get in his van and drive to a motel in Barstow. I sit here in the van, let Robert settle in. After a short time, I remove my things and myself from the van and head into the room. I set my things down and sit next to Robert, still unsure how to continue this relationship. Maybe we both need this quiet time. Suddenly, as if intended, the room starts to shake. I stare at Robert, who stares back at me, and grip his hand. Little crashes are happening around the room as things fall to the floor. It sounds like a war zone outside with all of the car sirens and police sirens going. This is where I thrive. The disaster is where I belong. The thought of hurting Robert and getting off on an earthquake hurts me to my core. I can't hold back tears. I need to connect with him, and I need to connect with myself.

"Can we take your van into the desert?" I ask. He asks me what I'm talking about. "I want to spend some time in seclusion. I want to spend some time in seclusion with you." For me, this is my brain's way to get back into us. "I don't know," he says. It breaks my heart. "Please think about it." He stands and heads outside for a cigarette. I look at him through the window. He comes up to the glass and says he's going to find us coffee. I know he'll be back. I know him.

The Passion

I wonder what's going through Robert's head. I really do. I think I'm in love with him, even though my shrink would tell me that this is just not possible. Not possible why? Because you can't fall in love that quickly? How much time do we need if we don't have much time? I know Robert is in love with me. I also wonder if he hates me. I look at my phone. I look for a sign. There is nothing there, save for another twenty messages from Tommy. The diner has left me a message as well. I'm guessing it's simply to tell me I'm fired. I think about me and Robert going off into the desert. I think of scenes of a campfire and coffee like you see the old cowboys doing or like you see all over designer feeds. I can hear the coyotes howling. I can hear the snakes shuffling. I feel like the medicine that comes with the spirit of the desert will be good medicine. Speaking of medicine, it's time to take my pill. Shortly after taking it, though Robert is not here yet, I fall asleep.

The Painted Desert

I wake up before Robert. I will let him sleep. I decide to take a warm shower and relax my soul while he wakes. While in the shower, I hear the door to the motel room close. I wonder if he's left. I wonder if he's left for good. I wouldn't blame him for leaving. I step out of the shower and look at my distorted figure in the steamed mirror. I draw a heart on the mirror. I step out of the bathroom and start to get dressed. Robert comes into the room with coffee. He's still not really speaking to me, or with me, or whatever. Regardless, I can feel him scanning my body. He hands me my coffee and heads out to the van to wait for me to join him.

On the way to wherever we are going, Robert stops for gas and smokes. He asks me to get the essentials, and I do. As we pack our water and things into the van, I feel the ringing in my ears. I can hear an earthquake siren in the distance. I tell Robert I forgot something and head back toward the store. As I enter, I pull the gun out of my bag and point it at the clerk. His hands are slightly raised and he is shaking. I tell him to calm the fuck down and to put all the money into my bag. He struggles a little bit but manages to shove the drawer's contents where I ask.

"Stay put or I'll fucking kill you!" I yell as he cowers. "I mean it! Stay fucking cool."

I fast walk back to the van and say, "Let's go, man."

Robert rips out of the parking lot and onto Main. He drives cautiously while I decompress. Nobody followed us, at least not that I can tell. I'm not sure anyone was paying attention to us anyway. Sirens and alarms do strange things to people's psyche. Their awareness goes to shit. They attribute everything to the noise, figure it's taken care of, and move on with their business.

"This is it!" I shout to Robert. We are at a crossroads. The crossroad itself is a desert dirt road. It looks like it leads into nowhere, exactly where we need to be.

"I love you." I don't know why just said that. It just came out of me. I do, though. I love him. I know he loves me too. This is why we need this. This is also why I can't hurt him. He can't hurt me or maybe he can. I will hurt him. I wish it wasn't so.

After some distance, Robert parks the van at the base of a small hill. "Let's go," I say as I hop out of the van.

"Right here," Robert places his sheets and blankets onto a soft patch of sand.

We both forage for wood to burn. I find some bushes and

shrubs and Robert shows up with an armful of old boards. This guy, what the fuck?

He places a larger piece of wood on the small fire and sits next to me. He lights a cigarette. I need to break our silence. I need him right now. "I'm sorry," Is all I can say.

Robert asks me what I hit him with. I wanted to say that I hit him with Cupid's mother-fucking arrow but instead tell him the truth.

He asks me if I robbed the gas station. Again, I tell him the truth. I put a pile of bills in his hand and pull out a bottle of tequila that the clerk at the gas station had generously thrown in. I take a drink and hand the bottle to Robert. I watch him take a drink before I, with all the passion I can muster up, kiss him. I pull away and continue to stare into his eyes. That's what it took. He grabs me by the back of my head and tears me apart. Afterward, he continues to sip on the tequila. I can feel the sun fade and I can feel Robert fade. He is swirling. I want to tell him I love him. I want to love him. We are naked in the desert with a small fire, a little pile of money, and a bottle of tequila. I feel his fluids inside me as I look to the Milky Way. I feel him lying next to me.

The Night

I lay there, looking into his eyes. The moon and the stars cast a cool glow about everything. It's very cold, so I put some more wood on the fire. Robert drank a lot of tequila and is passed out hard. Minutes seem like hours. Surrounded by the silence, hills silhouette the sky, I can't do this. The fact that we became this earthquake in the desert means it's going to distort. This relationship will turn ugly. He will control me, I know it. I'm already controlling him. Mom, what should I do? I know what you'd do. Fuck him again. I kind of want to fuck him again. I cover him up, place some of the money in his bag, and drop some more wood on the fire. I look at his face and the necklace. I take the necklace and kiss him softly. I take his van and leave.

Part 3

Winslow, Arizona

Not California

After waking up and finding the van gone, I started walking back toward the main road—the Mother Road. Every now and then, the earth would tremble a little as I walked. My soul was completely destroyed and my heart was completely destroyed. My whole being was broken. This meant that I wasn't thinking about Crystal or anything. I nearly froze to death that night and am now baking in the sun.

I come up to a set of railroad tracks. I stand on them facing east. I think about just standing here until a train comes and removes me from this earth at high speed. My mother's necklace is gone. I can feel the train unless it's just another earthquake.

I step off the track and the train begins to pass. Suddenly, as if lifted by a breeze, I'm hanging off one of the boxcar's ladders. I'm familiar with a boxcar because we had one in the woods by my house growing up. All of us kids played on it until we were old enough to smoke dope in it. I move myself around the side and into the car. We are heading east. I sit down in the car. Even if I had slept for twenty hours, I'd still be tired.

All I wanted to do was head out west. Do the head-out-west thing. I would have gotten a job and worked in a box and rewarded myself with smokes and coffee and stayed there until I couldn't. I'm guessing that the benefit would be the weather. No more smoking in the snow. Of course, I'd probably be trading it in for smoking in a wildfire. Maybe that's north. Either way, instead, I'm in a train car, no van, almost out of money, and I'm in love with the girl who took it all from me. I think about all these things as we pass back into Arizona. Closer, not further, from Ashton.

I check my phone. I've got nothing going on there. Pics of the guys from the office, celebrating my departure. I can't look for Crystal; I'm not even sure that is her name. I'm not sure I know anything about her.

Through the reservation, I can feel the earthen structures dry out my spirit. There are some dogs. They look like they've had a rough life.

Several more hours pass. A couple of towns and cities pass. I see a sign for Winslow and decide to depart. I'm hungry and tired and need a break from this hobo bullshit.

I jump off at Williamson Ave and walk toward what I think is the town. Immediately, I find a bar and grill. I notice some people getting their picture taken by a statue up ahead. My curiosity trumps my hunger, and I walk up to take a look. I'm standing on the corner in Winslow, Arizona. I know this because the mural on the wall above tells me so. Maybe this is a sign. Take it easy.

That's what the sign across the street says.

Looking in the direction of the *Take it Easy* sign, my heart drops. The same building with those Buddhist-sounding words has a small parking lot in front of it. I can see the taillights of my van peeking out from behind a wall.

My fucking van.

Still not California

I approach the van with caution. I either don't want her to leave, or I don't want her to leave. Basically, I'm fucking dying, and I need to know why. It's like I can feel her energy. My nerves burn, and my heart is heavy. I almost can't walk at all. I get up to the van and can't see anyone inside. I duck into the alleyway. I'm going to fucking wait here until she shows. I light a smoke. I think about lighting myself on fire. I'm watching people take their picture with a statue of Jackson Browne or the Eagles or some fucking thing. I may as well melt into the fucking concrete. I only have *one woman on my mind.*

I catch my reflection in the window. I look older and distorted. I'm a fucking mess, maybe a train wreck is a more suitable way to say it. I think about when I first got the van. Me and some buddies were gonna have a band. We were going to tour all over hell and all over Ohio. We wanted to be rock stars. We played shitty-sounding alternative music. We were kind of like Soundgarden but nothing like Soundgarden. Our singer was too far into the idea of all the rock star bullshit. He nearly drank himself to death in his brooding Morrison poetry. His version of Hemingway was not a way for him to act. He simply could not fucking handle it. He also was no rock star. After his girlfriends left him, he left for Portland. I got to keep the van, for a small fee. I performed the appropriate rituals in which to expel his evil spirits from the ride. I used the appropriate chemicals in which to disinfect his love potions from the seats. "Don't let the sound of your own wheels drive you crazy." Or something like that. I wonder what the fuck he's doing now. I'm not so sure I care.

I wonder what the fuck Crystal is doing in Winslow. How come she didn't go to California? Seems like she has nothing to lose at this point. I feel like I can still smell her on me. Fuck, I could smell her on me all the way from Barstow.

It's probably been a full hour that I'd been waiting for the next tremor. I feel my stomach begin to eat itself. I think it's time to stop worrying and get my shit together.

I light up a smoke and head over to the van as though I hadn't been hiding in an alley for what felt like a century. I look inside the driver's side window. I don't see any bodies. The door is unlocked, so I let myself in. She had taken the keys with her. Some of the supplies we had purchased for our camping trip are still where they were. There is a prescription bottle in the center console. The name on the bottle reads the name "Crystal O'Brien." I guess she didn't give me a bullshit name. I actually think that it's fucked up she didn't.

I pull out my phone to start looking up information on Crystal O'Brien and see what these pills are. I don't get very far. Suddenly, and heavily, I'm startled by the passenger door.

I look up; it's Crystal. She is stepping up and settling into the passenger seat. It's almost as though we had driven here together, and nothing had happened. In that brief few seconds, my whole body became warm and thrown into shock. I'm melting into the seat and onto the floor as though all of hell has encompassed my body after a lifetime of making shitty Devil deals. She's not looking at me; she's looking at the floor. I am looking directly into her. She can feel this. Finally, her little head turns toward me, and she looks into my soul. I know exactly what this means. I guess I can see the future again because I see this all playing out with us on the road again, fucking and singing and acting like nothing ever happened.

"I needed to get a refill," she says. "I need to find a pharmacy that can give me a refill."

I realized that I still had her prescription bottle in my hand. "You came to Winslow for a refill?"

"I came to Winslow because I can't go to California."

"Why can't you go to California?"

"Because I won't survive in California because if I do, it will fucking devour me. California is a dream, Javier. Don't you see? It's not a real place. It's a fantasy that's persisted for decades. It's no different than Oz or Fantastica. It's make-believe, imaginary. Robert, I already live in the imaginary, and you already live in the imaginary. How can we go to California, Javier? It'd be like running into yourself. We'd both melt in California! Not only that, but I love you. If we went to California, it would be a death sentence for us. Don't you see? If we went to California, we would become one, and our one would become our death. I can't be responsible for this, Robert. I know you understand. You can't be responsible for this either."

I do understand. Every fucking word that is coming out of her mouth, I understand. By going to California together, we are trapping each other in a dream, with the potential to become a nightmare. We would probably find a way to blame each other for the outcome. By her leaving, she's proactively saving us from a nuclear war. She's creating a cold war. The kind of cold war that can only be possible by nations so strong, with so much power, that without the cease-fire, would be total annihilation.

"I do understand. Crystal, I also know that I'm hungry and that you need your medicine. Could we do something here? I mean, something crazy?"

"What is it, Robert?"

"Let's find a motel and check-in. Let's get cleaned up and go get something to eat. Let's find you a pharmacy and take some time to breathe. I think we ended up letting ourselves get enveloped by that crazy earthquake. We fell into a crack in the earth and were lost. Let's take a minute to climb out of that crack and just exist."

"Yes."

"Give me the keys, Crystal."

She hands me the keys. I start the van, and Iggy's *Passenger* comes blaring through the speakers. I leave it on and leave it loud. I pull out of the parking lot and head down the road. Take it easy is what we are going to fucking do. I'm not saving her; she's not saving me. We are just going to exist as ourselves. No version of the future or its consequences will cross our minds.

Soap

I drive us a little bit west until we come up on a Quality Inn. I park in front of the lobby and take the keys in. I set us up with a room and park the van where I can see it. The two of us, our dwindling possessions, we walk hand-in-hand through the hotel and toward our room. I toss Crystal a granola bar and hand her a bottle of water. I take off my clothes and head into the shower. Not long after I get in, she joins me. She turns me and begins washing me. I follow her hair from her scalp to its ends, I'm attempting to give her the feeling you get when you get a wash in the salon. Our bodies, warm and slippery with soap, are pressed together. We let our demons wash down the drain. We get out, we dry each other off. I put my hand on her face and rub my thumb along her cheek. She does the same to me. We put on what is probably our last bit of clean clothes and head out of the room.

The van sits there in the parking lot all dusty and worn. I think about how it also needs a bath as I climb into the driver's seat. I'll need to find a car wash.

I drive us until we come to a place called Alonso's Mexican. Tacos seem right for the occasion, as opposed to Carl's Jr. or McDonald's. Ironically, Alonso's looks like it might have at one time been a McDonald's or Carl's. We order a half-dozen tacos and some sodas and find a place to sit. Our balloon feels deflated, yet it still floats.

"What did you do with my necklace," I ask her. There is a lot to talk about, but that necklace is important to me. I feel it is as good a dinner conversation as anything else.

She pulls down her shirt. "I put it on when we got dressed. I don't know why I took it. I feel its power. Perhaps, in a way, it is an extension of you."

"But you had me."

"And you had me."

"How are your tacos?"

"I'm eating them."

"After we eat, we'll stop at the Safeway across the street. Hopefully, they can get you your refill."

"Thank you."

"For what?"

"For listening."

"To what?"

"Just, thank you. That's all."

"Crystal, we are going to run out of money soon."

"I know. Can we just have today? Can we just do normal things today? We can worry tomorrow. Robert, I need a rest. I need us to rest."

"I'm sorry, that is the plan, isn't it. Let's get some Café Mochas after we eat. We'll wait for them to fill your prescription and look around. I don't know anything about this town, but it might be fun."

"I'd love to do that with you, Bob."

"Robert." We both kind of laugh.

We finish our food and head over to the Safeway. She gives them her prescription and asks for a rush on it. "I always ask for a rush on it," she says.

There is a Coffee House across the street. We know it is a coffee house because the sign on the side of the building literally says, "CoffeeHouse". We order our drinks. As we pay, the barista says, "Happy New Year." I look at my phone and realize that it's New Year's Eve. This is how our lives have been. No fucking clue what dimension we are in. I show Crystal the date, and her eyes light up.

"Oh my god, Robert. We have to celebrate a little bit or something. We have to kiss at midnight! I don't want you to kiss me; I don't want to kiss you; I want to kiss each other."

"It's a date. Let's check out this town and find our place."

On the wall, right by the exit to the Coffee House, is a flyer. "Standing on the Corner New Year's Eve Party."

I pull the flyer off of the wall and hand it to Crystal. "Free to all. Live Music. Jack Rabbit Drop."

"This is perfect," Crystal says. I can feel her excitement.

After we leave the coffee shop, Crystal runs into the Safeway and grabs her medication. It only takes her a minute. When she returns, I tell her that I think we need to get some clothes for the party tonight. She agrees and we head to a strip mall with some clothing stores.

We spend a couple of hours playing with each other and trying on clothes. We take advantage of the sample cologne and perfume. We don't have enough money for most anything right now. I mean, we have some but should probably not spend it.

We both emerge from separate dressing rooms in what we would consider New Year's Eve ensembles.

"You look beautiful," I tell her.

"You're not so bad-looking yourself," She replies. "Common,

let's go!"

She takes my hand and runs me out of the doors of the store. An alarm sounds as we run at full speed toward a group of cars at the north end of the parking lot. A clerk was on the sidewalk looking for the culprit. We wait until they head back in, and we weave and dodge between cars until we reach the van. Without anyone seeing us, we are out of the parking lot. We are both high. We are both lucid-high.

"You're a natural," she says. "Where have you been all my life? With you around, we could have robbed Fort Knox!"

"With me around, we'd both be in jail." We both laugh. "By the way, you look fucking great, Crystal. You always look great."

With a more serious look, she looks at me and says, "I think you're pretty great."

With those words, Kingman, the train, the desert, they are all behind me. With those words, I'm all in.

Auld Lang Syne

We arrive at a small park with an amphitheater, right next to the statue of the hippie guitar player. There are strings of lights, food trucks, a beer tent, and a DJ playing all sorts of music. Crystal and I head over to the beer tent and get a drink. Her face is glowing; she's a little flush from both the fun and the cold air. I can't stop looking at her face. I want to look at it forever.

The song *Celebration* comes through the loudspeakers. Crystal looks at me, "Come on, let's go!" She drags me out to the dance floor. I feel loose and warm and have no trouble awkwardly dancing with her. She's moving and shaking and throwing me winks. I can't believe this is happening.

The song ends, and we head to a wire spool that was made into a makeshift table. There are small fire pits placed around the park, and we are near one of them. She faces her palms to the flame and blows warm air into her fists.

"I'll be right back," I tell her before heading over to the DJ. I ask him if he could play R.E.M.'s *Nightswimming*. "I love that song, sure thing!" I head back to Crystal and take her hand. "What's up?" she asks. "It's a surprise," I say.

I lead her out to the dance floor, and the song starts to play.

A tear sheds itself from her eye as she takes my hand and pulls me close. We swim around in each other; our surroundings disappear. We look into each other's eyes and kiss. We kiss and swirl through the entire song. Cliché as it sounds, there is magic in the air. I look at her and see her as though through a camera lens. She is focused against the blur of the strings of lights, embers from the fires, people smiling, and celebrating.

We stroll back to our spool table. Suddenly, the music stops. The crowd stands, and we stand. The DJ announces that it's almost time for the jackrabbit drop. They are hoisting a crudely drawn but lit-up jackrabbit up a flagpole.

"I'd like to announce, to help us bring in the new year, our very own, WHS marching band!" The crowd cheers before the place goes silent. A few of the drummers from the band start a drum roll. The DJ is looking at his watch. He begins the countdown. "Ten – nine – eight," all while a man lowers the jackrabbit down the pole. "Seven – six – five," the drum roll is getting louder. "Four – three – two," Crystal looks me in the eyes, and I look into hers. "One!" The DJ and the crowd yell Happy New Year and begin singing Auld Lang Syne. Fireworks start going off while Crystal and I, still staring into each other, start kissing.

I feel her twitch and slightly fall as if she had stepped barefoot on a stone. I pull her gently up and notice that she has a small amount of blood spilling between her lips. She looks at me, her eyes have concern. She starts to fall, while in my arms. I lower her to the ground and look around. Others are fleeing, and some are staying. Some are screaming, and some are on the ground. The music is no longer playing. They are shining flashlights into the windows of the surrounding buildings. The fireworks are still going off.

I lean down to Crystal and put my hand on her. Her stomach is warm with blood.

"What the fuck happened?" She quietly asks. Similar to our night swim, the entire place disappears. It is just her and I in this moment. "I don't know, Crystal, something has gone terribly wrong. I think you've been shot. You're bleeding."

"Please kiss me," she asks. I place my lips on hers. "It's no matter, Robert. You see, I didn't have but a few months to live. I have cancer. No coin flip can determine this fate, Javier. This is why I kept leaving, it's why I kept your necklace. Robert, I didn't want you to lose me like that." She finds my hand and places my necklace into my palm. Tears fall from my face and onto her cheek. "I don't want to lose you at all," I say. "It's going to be okay. Help will come." I press my lips to hers as the life leaves her body. I collapse onto her, next to her, around her. I'm with her for what seems like an eternity. An eternity would not be long enough.

I'm pulled away by paramedics but can't hear anything. I think I'm screaming. I know I can't walk. They wrap me in a blanket and sit me down. I watch them performing CPR on her body. I watch them do what they do. I see them cover her with a sheet. I run back to her and lay with her. I realize what she said, however hard to think. I realize that this is how she wanted to go. Like this. I was an unexpected twist in her life. She is sleeping before me; her lips are smiling slightly.

I kiss her one last time.

Epilogue

Happy New Year

I stood there, staring up at a wall that divides the United States from Mexico. Stood there forever, on a mountain, separating the United States from Canada. Alone in both locations, and both require a long distance to return to people. The trips are in and of themselves necessary. I realize what Crystal was doing while she was running. She was living. I realized that I could never return to Camp Ashton, or any camp for that matter. No reward system could serve as enough to keep me in line.

Nope! Instead, I've become the hobo on the train, I've become the hippie on the corner, I've become the keeper of Crystal's spirit. For whatever it's worth, I'm free for it. I carry her with me, everywhere I go. I carry the pendant. I know she knew what she was doing there. She ended up connecting herself to me with it. It is the way she lives on with me.

Back in Winslow, it turns out it took them something like 25 minutes to have the shooter in custody. They found him in a backyard, underneath somebody's camper. He killed 3 people and injured 14. He has been sentenced to death by lethal injection sometime later this year. I intend to visit him. I feel it's necessary.

As far as the old van is concerned, she still gets me where I'm going without any problems. When I'm in it, I can still see her sitting in the seat, singing R.E.M. and experiencing the wind running around her face. I can still smell her, feel her, hear her voice whispering the words, "I think you're pretty great."

End.

About the Author

An Escanaba, Michigan native and life-long creative, Aaron Paul Schaut is the author of These Americans, These Americans - Short Stories, and Modern Clothing. When he's not scribbling his disjointed thoughts, he's writing music for Dynaflo, and riding a motorcycle all over hell.

More to Discover

Check out the *These Americans* series from author Aaron Paul Schaut.

Follow along on Kindle Vella with *These Americans: Short Stories* and a continuous collection of poems in *Modern Clothing*.

Dig into the books from *Starlite Pulp*. Dig into all of them.

Visit aaronschaut.com for more.